P9-CQR-738

Arnold's Valentine

Based on the TV series *Hey Arnold!*® created by Craig Bartlett as seen on *Nickelodeon*®.

No part of this publication may be reproduced in whole or in part, or stored in a retrieval system, or transmitted in any form or by any means, electronic, mechanical, photocopying, recording, or otherwise, without written permission of the publisher. For information regarding permission, write to Simon Spotlight, an imprint of Simon & Schuster Children's Publishing Division, 1230 Avenue of the Americas, New York, NY 10020.

ISBN 0-439-27622-5

Copyright © 2001 by Viacom International Inc. All rights reserved. NICKELODEON, *Hey Arnold!*, and all related titles, logos, and characters are trademarks of Viacom International Inc. Published by Scholastic Inc., 555 Broadway, New York, NY 10012, by arrangement with Simon Spotlight, an imprint of Simon & Schuster Children's Publishing Division. SCHOLASTIC and associated logos are trademarks and/or registered trademarks of Scholastic Inc.

12 11 10 9 8 7 6 5 4 1 2 3 4 5 6/0

Printed in the U.S.A.

First Scholastic printing, January 2001

NICKELODEON

HEY ARNOLD!™

Arnold's Valentine

by Craig Bartlett and Maggie Groening

based on a screenplay by
Steve Viksten and Rachel Lipman

interiors illustrated by Tim Parsons
cover illustrated by Tuck Tucker,
Kenji Notani, and Teale Wang

SCHOLASTIC INC.
New York Toronto London Auckland Sydney
Mexico City New Delhi Hong Kong

CHAPTER 1

"Check this out, Gerald." Arnold held up a large, red, lacy, glittery, angel-strewn valentine. "What do you think? I stayed up practically all night making it."

Gerald gave a low whistle. "Man, that is some piece of work."

"Oh, Arnold, you're way ahead of us!" Miss Slovak's voice came ringing from the front of the classroom. "That's just what we're all going to do today!" She said as she beamed at the fourth-grade class.

"Now, because it's Valentine's Day—and in keeping with our heart theme unit—we're going to make a valentine for someone we care about." She smiled radiantly at the blank faces. "Any questions? Good. Let's get going."

The kids set to work with red and white paper, lacy paper doilies, and large amounts of glue and glitter. All except Helga, who just chewed her pencil anxiously. She stared at the bright red paper heart in front of her. Then she wrote, *Arnold, Be my valentine. Sincerely, Helga.*

She studied it for a few seconds, then frowned. "'Sincerely?' Yeah, *that's* romantic. . . ."

She quickly erased and wrote again. *Arnold, Be my valentine. Or else.*

She studied the card, then erased again. *Dear football head . . .*

Helga grabbed her head with both hands and moaned. "Naw . . ." She erased so fiercely that the red paper tore.

"Oh, criminey! Stupid Valentine's Day. I HATE it!" She looked over to where Arnold was sitting, two rows away, and sighed as she eavesdropped on him.

"Gerald, tell me how this sounds," Arnold said. "'I have long admired you from afar, and now . . . I'd, uh, like to admire you from up close. Please meet me at Chez Pierre tonight at six o'clock.'"

Gerald shook his head admiringly. "You got some guts, Arnold."

Arnold smiled as he finished writing. "'Signed, Anonymous,'" he said.

Gerald rolled his eyes. "I guess I spoke too soon. You gotta *sign* it, man. How's she gonna know who 'Anonymous' is?"

"She'll just know, Gerald."

As Arnold held up his finished valentine to admire it, Helga stiffened. She could read the large letters on Arnold's card: *TO RUTH*.

"'TO RUTH'? Ruth? What does he want with HER?" Helga's grip tightened on her pencil as she muttered to herself. "She's nothing but a stuck-up, sixth-gradey, training-bra-wearing, bracey-faced, sixth-gradey . . . sixth grader! The thought of them together makes me—" The pencil snapped in two. "AGGHHH!" Helga hurled the pieces into the wastebasket.

Miss Slovak frowned disapprovingly at Helga, then addressed the class. "Now class, time to *neatly* put away our supplies. And while we're doing that, I'll hand out the latest letters from our overseas pen pals!" She reached into the mailbag on her desk. "Here's one for Rhonda. . . ."

She pulled out a heart-shaped box. "Looks

like another package of gourmet chocolates from Paolo in Italy!"

Helga sighed. "I never get any fancy presents from *my* pen pal."

"Don't worry, Helga," said Miss Slovak. "Sometimes the most beautiful gift can come in the plainest box. Let's see what we have from *your* pen pal."

She dug around in the bottom of the mailbag, frowning. "Oh, here we are." Miss Slovak handed Helga a limp postcard. It showed a barren, brown desert with a single dry and sickly-looking tree. Helga flipped the card over. "'PLEASE SEND MONEY.' Yeah, right," she muttered. "Beautiful."

Miss Slovak pulled out a thick, bumpy, grease-spotted letter and held it at arm's length. "Arnold, here's another letter from your pen pal Cecile in France." She sniffed. "And it certainly seems . . . potent."

"Great," Arnold said. "I bet it's that blue cheese she promised."

Just then, the bell rang. Arnold laid the letter on his desk. "Guess I'll read it after recess." He headed out the door with Gerald.

CHAPTER 2

At recess, Helga slumped in a corner by herself, arms folded across her knees. She glowered across the playground at Ruth, who sat at a picnic table, sorting through a pile of valentines. Suddenly, Arnold snuck up behind Ruth and slipped his valentine into her pile.

Then he ducked behind a tree and watched eagerly as Ruth opened his valentine, read it, and smiled mysteriously.

Helga slapped her forehead. "Crimíney! Not only is Arnold mooning over that idiotic sixth grader, but he's got that *baguette*-eating so-and-so Cecile writing him fancy letters! What am I gonna do?" she muttered. "I've got *no one*, and he's got *two* valen—"

Helga stopped. She blinked twice, then smiled slowly. "Wait a minute. Hold the phone. If he wants *two* valentines, I'll give him two. . . ." She chuckled. Then she jumped up and sneaked into the school.

Alone in the classroom, Helga went straight to Arnold's desk and opened the letter from his pen pal. Chunks of white, blue-veined cheese fell to the floor. She took a step back from the mess and began to read.

"'Dear Arnold, How are you? Everything is . . .' hmm . . . 'tress-bean here in France. I am sending you some *bleu* cheese . . .' blah, blah, blah, who cares." Helga looked around and seized a pen from a nearby desk. "Now, to implement my brilliant plan."

She hunched over the letter and wrote, *P.S. I am coming to visit you in the United States, and I want to meet you on Valentine's Day at . . .*

Helga paused and thought. "Oh criminey, what was that restaurant where Arnold wanted Ruth to meet him at? Chez Padoo? Chez Paroo? Uh, Chez Paris. Yeah, that's it. . . . 'Chez Paris.'" She studied her effort. "Perfect." Helga put the letter back in its envelope and laid it on Arnold's desk. "This is gonna get *fun*," she said, and ran back outside.

♡ ♡ ♡

Arnold read his pen pal's letter aloud as he and Gerald walked home that afternoon. When he got to the P.S., he stopped and stared in disbelief. "Oh, no! Cecile is flying into town with her parents, and she wants to meet me *tonight!* Gerald, help me!" Arnold pleaded.

"Yeah, right, Arnold, like you really need my help," Gerald said playfully. "You've got a Valentine's date with *not one,* but *two* girls, while I'll be stuck playing 'Got Your Nose' with my kid sister."

They continued walking. Arnold thought hard. They turned a corner, and Arnold stopped again. "Look, Gerald." He pointed at two restaurants. "It's so weird. I'm meeting Ruth at Chez Pierre, and right across the street is the other restaurant where Cecile wants to meet me, Chez Paris."

Gerald looked from one restaurant to the other and then back again. He smiled. He had an idea.

"Okay, Arnold. I got it. Here's what you do. You set up tables in both restaurants, and

CHEZ PIERRE
PIERRE
Chez Paris

if Ruth doesn't show up—and believe me, she won't—you're cool. If she *does*, you can make an excuse and go across the street."

Arnold followed Gerald's gaze from one restaurant to the other. He smiled. "Gerald, it just might work."

CHAPTER 3

Helga ran all the way home. When she got there, she closed the front door behind her and leaned against it, thinking furiously. "Okay, Step One accomplished. Now for Step Two." She turned and ran up the stairs to her room.

Rummaging through her cassette tapes, she plucked one out and shoved it into her tape player. Then she ran to her closet and began quickly picking through her clothes.

"I gotta find something that makes me look French." Helga grabbed a lime-green knit dress and held it up, checking the effect in the mirror. "Hmm . . . 'Hello, boys and girls, I'm the lunch lady.' This won't do!" She threw it on the floor and continued her search.

The tape began to play. A cheerful voice filled the room. "*Bonjour.* And welcome to *So You Want to Speak French*. I am your teacher, *Monsieur Tavernier.*"

Helga held up a blouse with puffy sleeves and tiny clown faces all over it. It immediately joined the pile on the floor. She plunged deeper into the closet. When she emerged she was dragging a striped dress with long sleeves. "Hmm. A few alterations, and this just might work."

♡ ♡ ♡

Up in his attic room, Arnold paced back and forth. "What am I going to say to her, Gerald?"

"You gotta have some kind of speech prepared," Gerald said from his relaxed position flat out on the couch. "You can't just walk in there and babble. Ruth's an older woman; she'll think you're a goofball."

"Right, right. So what should I say?"

"Well, what do you know about her?"

Arnold thought for a moment, and his face softened into a dreamy smile. "Well, she's tall and delicate. And she has this really shiny auburn hair that just kind of cascades over her ears. And soft, brown eyes that sparkle somehow, and—"

"Arnold, are you trying to make me puke?" Gerald said.

"Huh?" Arnold shook his head, letting go of the vision. "Oh, sorry, Gerald. It's just, when I think about her, I feel sort of . . . floaty."

Gerald stood up and took Arnold by the

shoulders, giving him a firm shake. "Get a hold of yourself. Look, all that stuff is just what you *see*. What do you really *know* about Ruth?"

"Well, I . . . I know she's . . . um . . ." Arnold looked blank. "Huh. I guess I really don't know much about her. I just want to tell her how much I like her."

Gerald sighed loudly. "This is gonna be even harder than I thought. Listen, you're gonna have to come in slow; find out some things about her: hobbies, her favorite color, deep stuff like that. And then build to the big moment, where you tell her, you know"—he winced—"the yucky stuff."

Arnold sat down, and Gerald started pacing. "Now, let's plan out some speeches in case you freeze up."

"Okay . . ." Arnold thought for a minute. "Okay, how's this? 'Ruth, I know you don't really know me—'"

"'And *I* don't really know *you* . . . ,'" added Gerald.

"Right, right." Arnold waved him to be quiet. "'But for the past few months I've watched you from afar, and I think you're really pretty. And you have a nice smile. And once I saw you give up your seat on the bus to an old lady carrying a watermelon.'"

Gerald perked up a little. "Hey, that's good."

"'And . . . it probably sounds dumb, but whenever I think about you, I get all . . . floaty. I guess what I'm trying to say is . . . I really like you. And I think you're . . .'" Arnold paused and looked sheepishly over at Gerald. "You're gonna puke, right?"

Gerald didn't answer right away.

"Gerald?"

"It's beautiful, man. Don't change a thing." He sighed. "Let's go get you dressed."

CHAPTER 4

Helga's new French look was coming together. She hardly looked like herself at all. Her striped dress with the oddly cut, asymmetrical sleeves trailed behind her as she clumped along the sidewalk in her big sister Olga's smart, but slightly too large, high-heeled shoes.

"Now, my hair. What to do about my hair . . ." Then she spotted a store sign: JOLIE CHIEN SALON.

JOLIE CHIEN
SALON
SAL

"That's the ticket. Just what I need, a French hair salon." She headed for the store. "Real French, that's the look. Whatever froufrou, la-di-da business they're wearing in Paris."

As Helga looked through the window, a woman emerged carrying two yapping, freshly groomed French poodles.

♡ ♡ ♡

Arnold and Gerald found an ancient tuxedo in a rarely opened boardinghouse closet. It fit Arnold pretty well. "Man, you are *sharp*. You could be a waiter," Gerald said admiringly.

"I couldn't have done this without you, Gerald," Arnold said, checking his watch. "Well, I gotta go. Wish me luck."

"You won't need luck. Just remember everything I told you."

Arnold and Gerald did their secret

handshake. It didn't make Arnold feel more confident, but it did help him feel like he still had a friend. He turned and headed for Chez Paris.

♥ ♥ ♥

When Helga emerged from the Jolie Chien Salon three hours later, her once-blond hair was pale pink, and her stiff pigtails had been permed and shaped into two pink puffballs that stuck out like a poodle's ears on both sides of her head. Her pink bangs hung poofily over one eye.

Helga glanced at her reflection in the window. "Oh well, they say it's the rage in Paris. . . ." She shrugged. "Whatever." She checked her watch. "Oh, my gosh, I'll be late to meet my beloved!"

As she clomped along in slightly-too-big shoes, she smiled dreamily. "Now my plan comes together. Not only will I be snatching my beloved Arnold from the clutches of that dopey, air-brained, sixth-grade yo-yo Ruth, but I will finally get to express my true feelings to him of the football-shaped head, for whom I so long have pined!" She sighed romantically. "And the best part is, there's *no risk* involved. Arnold won't even know it's me. All he'll see is Cecile. Boy, what a great plan. *Nothing* can go wrong."

♡ ♡ ♡

Meanwhile, flying high above the Atlantic Ocean, a nine-year-old girl was so excited that the only thing keeping her from dancing on the chair was her seat belt. She stared eagerly out the window at the clouds, then turned to her father.

"Oh, Papa, I am so happy," the girl said. "After so long writing letters back and forth, tonight I will finally meet my wonderful American pen pal, Arnold."

Her father smiled at her. "Ah, *oui*, Cecile. I am so happy for you, too. Just think of the look on Arnold's face when you surprise him with your visit!"

CHAPTER 5

At the Chez Paris restaurant, Arnold waited nervously at a table for two near the door. He folded and refolded his napkin into something sort of like a swan, in between checking his watch and glancing at the door. He studied his photo of Cecile for the fourth time. Just as he was putting it away, someone called his name.

"Arnold, over here! I mean, bone-sewer, ooh-la-la!"

Arnold looked at the pink-haired girl waving to him. He stood up. "Uh . . . Cecile? It's great to finally meet you." He took out the photo and stared. "Gee, you don't look much like your picture."

Helga snatched the photo away. "I don't? I mean, uh, *comme ci, comme ça,* whaddaya know?" She laughed nervously as she tore the photo to shreds behind her back.

"And your accent . . . ," said Arnold. "It's so . . . American."

"Yes, *oui,* I have been working on my English, ooh-la-la," Helga said.

They sat down, and Helga tried to bury her head in her menu. Arnold studied her carefully. Finally she put down the menu and glared at him. "What? What is it?"

Arnold shook his head. "There's just . . . something about you . . . I almost feel like I know you already."

Helga tugged her poofy pink bangs a little lower over her face. "That's impossible, mercy boo-coo. We've never met. Never seen each other before. Ever. Ooh-la-la."

Arnold blinked, a little taken aback. "I know. I meant . . . from your letters."

Helga swallowed. "Oh, right! My letters, ha ha ha . . . *quelle fromage.*" She ducked behind the menu again.

"So, tell me more about your life in France," said Arnold. "I have so many questions."

"France? Ah, well, Paris is quite a city. Big and busy, and . . . full of French people. Ooh-la-la!"

Arnold looked confused. "Paris? But I thought you lived on a farm in the Loire Valley."

"A farm? Ah, *oui oui*. My farm. How could I forget my lovely farm?" She looked stricken.

"And how are the goats doing? And your friend Monique? Is she still—"

Helga was starting to panic. "Ah, *oui*, of course—mercy boo-coo. But enough about me. Let's talk about *you*. How do you like your school, uh, what is it called again—P.T. 109?"

"Actually, it's P.S. 118," Arnold said. "And it's pretty good, I guess."

"And how about your class? Do you like the other students?"

"Sure."

Helga leaned forward. "Is there anyone you especially *like* in your class? Perhaps a smart, funny, beautiful, interesting . . . girl?"

Arnold thought hard. "Hmm, I've never really thought about it. Let's see . . . beautiful, huh? Smart?" He shook his head, stumped.

Helga drummed her nails on the table. "Perhaps not necessarily beautiful, but possessing a certain *je ne sais quoi*?"

Arnold looked at her doubtfully. "I'm not sure I know anyone who has one of those."

Helga shook her head impatiently. "Arnold, what I want to ask you is . . ."

Arnold glanced out the window at Chez Pierre, the restaurant across the street. Ruth had just walked up! He could see her standing near the door. Arnold turned back to Cecile. "Excuse me a minute. I have to go to the—"

"Ah, *oui oui*," Helga said.

"Exactly." Arnold walked quickly from the table. When he got to the exit, he glanced back to check that Cecile wasn't watching. Then he bolted across the street.

Helga didn't notice. She was already rehearsing for Arnold's return. "Arnold, I have to tell you . . . I . . . love . . . I like . . . I'm in like . . . I'm deeply in . . . like . . . oh, I'm *never* going to say it!" She slapped her forehead. "Pull yourself together, Helga, I mean, Cecile . . . I mean, Helga . . . criminey, I'm a basket case!"

CHAPTER 6

Arnold paused in the doorway of Chez Pierre to catch his breath. Then he went over to Ruth.

"Excuse me, I'm looking for—," she said.

"You're here! You made it!" Arnold exclaimed.

"Yeah," Ruth said. "I'm looking for a Mr."—she checked Arnold's valentine—"Anon-y-mous? Party of two?"

"Yeah, yeah, the table's all ready! Right

this way." Arnold guided her over to a window table and took a quick glance at his other date sitting in the window of Chez Paris across the street. Cecile appeared to be waiting patiently, her head resting on the plate in front of her.

Arnold pulled Ruth's chair out for her. "Here, sit, sit down. Would you like some water or something?"

"I'll have a Yahoo soda."

Arnold glanced across the street again. Cecile was now making wild hand gestures to herself. He decided he'd better get back over there.

"Great, good choice. Listen, I'll be right back. You . . . stay right there and eat some bread sticks and relax, I'll be back before you know it!" Ruth picked up the menu as Arnold dashed for the door. "Yeah, don't forget the straw, okay?" she called as he ran across the street.

A busboy approached her. "*Bonjour,* how ya doin'? Can I get you something to drink?"

Ruth looked up, startled. "I just ordered from that other busboy."

The busboy frowned. "What? This is *my* section!"

Ruth shrugged and turned back to her menu. "I hope this Anonymous guy isn't going to be real late."

Arnold ran panting back to his table at Chez Paris. "Sorry. The line for the bathroom was—whew!"

Helga looked up at him. "Ah, *oui.* So, Arnold, you were telling me about a girl in your class."

"A girl? There're lots of girls in my class." He laughed, then looked at her. "Well, there *is* this one girl, Helga . . ."

Helga gulped. She tried to look casual. "What do you notice especially? Ooh-la-la . . . ," she trailed off weakly.

"Well, she kind of"—Arnold groped for the right words—"I don't know. She bugs me sometimes."

Helga arched an eyebrow. "Oh?"

"Yeah. She bosses everyone around, and she just . . . bugs me."

"She 'bugs' you, eh?"

"Yeah, you know what 'bugs' means. Not crawly bugs, but—"

Helga forgot her Cecile voice for a moment and snapped, "I KNOW what 'bugs' means!" Then she caught herself. "I mean, mercy boo-coo!" She took a deep breath and smiled sweetly. "What I mean to say is, perhaps there is a *reason* why this one certain girl bugs you. Perhaps deep, *deep* down, Arnold, you really *like* her?" She looked hard at him, willing him to agree.

Arnold thought for a moment. "Deep, *deep* down, Cecile . . ."—he shrugged—"I'd have to say she *really* bugs me."

Helga sat back and sighed. "Well, at least you feel *something*." Then she leaned forward. "Arnold, there's something I have to tell you . . ."

"Yes?"

"I . . . that is, ooh-la-la . . . I know we haven't known each other that long, but, mercy boo-coo . . . I want to say . . . I like—I mean, Cecile . . . that's me, of course, I mean, I . . . like—" She groaned and slid way down in her chair.

Arnold leaned over and peered at her. "You all right down there? Listen, I'll be right back. I just want to . . . go wash up before we order. Okay?"

Cecile's voice came faintly from under the table. "Ah, *oui*, tress-bean, mercy boo-coo." As he walked away, Helga slowly pulled herself back up. "Oh, *criminey*!"

CHAPTER 7

Arnold dashed into Chez Pierre and threw himself into the chair opposite Ruth. "Hi," he panted. "Sorry I was gone so long."

"I already got a Yahoo from that other busboy," she said.

Arnold looked confused. "Busboy? Oh, you thought . . . no, I'm not the busboy. I'm"—he stopped and thought—"Let me put it this way. You're probably wondering about that valentine. About who 'Anonymous' really is."

"What do you think I am, dumb or something?" said Ruth. "Everyone knows who 'Anonymous' is."

"They *do*?"

"Yeah, he's, like, a famous poet."

"Huh?"

"Sure, every time we read a poem at school, half the time it's by that guy, Anonymous."

"Oh. Right." Arnold looked at her. Disappointment was creeping in. "Listen, Ruth, why don't we talk a little. I want to know *all* about you."

"Okay, but when this Anonymous guy shows up, you're going to have to go."

As it turned out, Ruth had no trouble sharing all about herself. Fifteen minutes later, Arnold found himself holding up his head with his hands as she chattered on.

" . . . so then in the third grade, that's

when I first started wearing my hair in *two* barrettes instead of one, okay?"

"You don't say." Arnold blinked. "Listen, Ruth—"

"But then, Jenny Stiletto starts going around with the same hairdo, like she thought of it first, can you believe that?"

"Incredible. Now that I've heard all about your hair, do you want to know anything about me?" Arnold asked.

"Yeah, sure, Alfred. What do *you* think of my hair?"

Arnold stared at her. "I think it's beautiful. But—" He looked across the street at Cecile. Then he got up. "Would you excuse me, please?"

Ruth handed him the empty breadbasket. "I'll have some more bread sticks?" Arnold took the basket. "I'll tell the busboy," he said with a sigh as he headed for the door.

Back at Chez Paris, Arnold threw himself back in his chair breathlessly. "Sorry about that, Cecile. The rest room—"

"Yeah, yeah, don't sweat it, I mean, uh, what matters is that now you're here, I'm here . . ." She noticed that Arnold looked troubled. "Is something wrong, Arnold?"

"No, nothing, it's just that . . ." He paused, then decided to tell Cecile how he was feeling. "Have you ever noticed that sometimes when you think you like a person from far away, you find out they're not what you thought they were when you get up close?"

"What do you mean?" Helga asked, tugging nervously at her pink bangs.

"Well, say, for instance, there's this girl I thought I liked, but then it turned out that when I got to know her, we had nothing in common."

"Maybe . . . she is not the girl . . . for you," Helga said carefully.

"Hmm . . . I'm starting to wonder."

"Maybe the girl for you is someone you didn't expect. After all, the most beautiful gift can come in the plainest box."

Arnold considered the thought. "You know, I think you're right. You have such a good way of putting things, Cecile."

Helga shrugged. "Just an old French expression."

Arnold smiled at her. She smiled back.

"I'm glad you came to visit me, Cecile. I'm having a great time with you tonight."

Helga blinked, amazed. She looked at him hopefully. "You are? Me too." She hesitated, then plunged ahead. "Arnold, there's something I really want to tell you. . . ."

"Yes?"

"Well, I . . . I really like, I mean, mercy

boo-coo, I really think that . . . I'm in LIKE with you. And I have to know. Do you . . . like me?"

"I, uh . . ." Arnold looked at her, then looked across the street. Ruth was still sitting there. Helga waited, and when Arnold didn't say anything, she asked, "Are you all right, Arnold?"

"Would you excuse me one last time? There's something I kinda have to take care of," Arnold said, jumping up. He looked at her earnestly. "But I'll be right back."

"What the heck is going on with him?" Helga muttered as Arnold dashed off again.

CHAPTER 8

Arnold rushed into Chez Pierre. Ruth was no longer alone. Tony the busboy had joined her.

"So," Tony said to Ruth, "You like gum?"

"Yeah," Ruth said.

"Me too! I *love* gum."

"Do you like my hair?" Ruth asked.

Tony leaned toward her. "I think it's awesome!"

"Me too!" They gazed at each other in perfect enchantment as they both reached for the last bread stick.

"Hey, want I should get us some more bread sticks?" Tony asked.

"I LOVE bread sticks!" Ruth said.

"Me TOO! Wanna go get some ice cream?"

Ruth nodded eagerly. As she and Tony got up, she finally noticed Arnold standing by the table. "Oh, hi, Alfred. We were just leaving. You can clear the table."

Arnold took a deep breath. "Listen, Ruth," he said. "I'm *not* the busboy. And I'm not Alfred. I'm ARNOLD!" He picked up the valentine Ruth had left on the table. "Before you go, I need you to know something. The truth is, I came here to say something to you tonight. I . . . I'm 'Anonymous.'"

"The *poet*?" she asked.

"I love your work!" said Tony.

Ruth turned to him. "Me too!"

"No, you don't get it," Arnold said. "I'm the one who sent you the valen—" He stopped when he saw how confused they both were. "I mean, yeah, that's right, I'm the poet. Have fun getting ice cream. You two belong together."

"Gee, thanks, Anonymous," Tony said, and he and Ruth turned to go.

Suddenly there was a loud bellow at the door of the restaurant. "ARNOLD!" yelled Helga. She blocked the doorway, forcing Tony and Ruth to edge around her. Then she marched toward Arnold.

"What the heck is going on here? I flew ten thousand miles just to have you two-time me? Well, excusay mwow!"

"Wait, Cecile, let me explain. I came here to have dinner with you, but I already had this other thing set up—"

"Don't bother, I've heard it all. *Comme çi, comme ca.*"

"But it's true!"

Helga poked a finger at Arnold's chest. "If there's one thing I can't stand, it's someone not being COMPLETELY HONEST about WHO THEY ARE!"

Just then, a pleasant-looking girl appeared in the doorway behind Helga, followed by a very anxious-looking Gerald. She looked around. "*Excusez-moi,* I am looking for Arnold?"

Arnold stepped forward. "Who are you?" he asked.

The *real* Cecile's face lit up. "Arnold?" She beamed. "I am Cecile! Surprise!"

CHAPTER 9

"Your *grandpapa* told me I would find you here," said the real Cecile. She paused, confused. "You do not recognize me from my photo?"

"*You're* Cecile? But you can't be Cecile, because"—Arnold pointed to Helga—"*she's* Cecile."

Helga tugged at her bangs. "Uh, yeah, that's right. *I'm* Cecile, the real Cecile, ooh-la-la, *Notre Dame*."

Cecile looked dismayed. "What is going on? *Je ne comprends pas*. I do not understand."

Gerald stepped forward and grabbed Arnold's arm. "Could I see you for a minute, Casanova?"

They stepped aside as the two Ceciles watched.

"Gerald, you got here just in time. I don't know what's going on, but—"

"Looks like what you've got here is one Cecile too many," Gerald whispered.

"You've gotta help me out. That girl who just walked in is the *real* Cecile. The Cecile I remember from the picture, anyway."

"Then who's the girl you just had dinner with?" Gerald asked, looking over at Helga.

"Beats me, but I had a great time! So I need you to do me a favor." Arnold whispered in Gerald's ear.

Gerald nodded. "Got it." He turned to the real Cecile. "Hi, how ya doin'? I'm Arnold."

"*You're* Arnold?" Cecile asked, confused.

Helga blinked, just as confused.

Gerald took the real Cecile by the arm and gently guided her out of the restaurant. "I'll explain it to you later," he said. "But for now, what do you say you and I get something to eat? I know a great hamburger joint down the street."

Cecile smiled. "Ah, *le* hamburger, an American *classique*! *Allons-y*, Arnold!"

Arnold watched them walk away, and Helga watched Arnold. Finally she spoke. "What a . . . crazy night, huh?"

Arnold looked at her. "You're not Cecile, are you?"

Helga shook her head, her lip trembling. "Nope."

"Then who *are* you?"

Helga looked down at her shoes. "I . . . can't tell you."

"Why not?"

She stamped her foot, almost in tears. "I just *can't*, okay?"

Arnold nodded slowly. "Okay. I don't have to know. I just want to tell you that this was the best Valentine's Day I ever had."

Helga looked shyly up at him. This was better than she could have dreamed: Arnold *liked* her, *and* he was letting her escape with her secret intact!

"Me too." She smiled. "You know, we really *did* have a great time together. But now, I have to go."

"Well," Arnold said, "we'll always have Chez Paris." He kissed Helga's hand. "Good-bye, Cecile."

Helga sighed. "Oh-re-vor, Arnold. Perhaps we will meet again someday." She turned to

go. Then she quickly slipped her feet out of the too-big shoes, picked them up, and ran down the street without looking back.

Arnold watched as Helga disappeared around the corner. "I hope so, valentine," he said.

about the authors

Hey Arnold! creator Craig Bartlett was born in Seattle, Washington. He wanted to grow up to be either an artist or a secret agent, but became an animator instead. He moved to Los Angeles in 1987 to direct the Penny cartoons for *PeeWee's Playhouse*. Craig stayed to write and direct on the first season of *Rugrats*, which introduced him to his friends at Nickelodeon. He premiered his first episode of *Hey Arnold!* on Nick in 1996, and has since made 100 episodes. He lives with his wife, Lisa, and kids, Matt and Katie, in Glendale, California, and enjoys painting, snorkeling, and reading the *New Yorker* magazine, preferably in Hawaii.

Maggie Groening was born in Portland, Oregon, where she grew up wanting to be a writer and watching a lot of TV. She moved to New York City in 1983, and worked as a writer for Children's Television Workshop, Disney, and many textbook companies. In 1991 she wrote the Maggie Simpson book series with her brother and co-author Matt Groening. She lives in Brooklyn, New York, with her husband, Potter; her children, Franklin and Louise; and a crabby cat.